Sandpiper Run

By Linda J Pifer

Published by Readingseat Books LLC US

The characters, events, or specific places in this book are fictitious. Any similarity to real persons living or dead is coincidental and not intended by the author.

Cover design and graphics by Damon Navari ©

Fine Art Illustrator/Graphic Artist

Library of Congress Control Number: 2019907985

ISBN 978-0-9890142-7-4

First Edition: August 2019

Other Books by Linda J Pifer

∞Ohio Girl∞

∞The Windows Trilogy∞
Windows
Daniel Smith - New Zealand Passage
Copperswift - Return to Highbridge

∞Thistle & Stone∞

To life with no fear
and faith like a
river.

Jinda

Chapter One - First Step

"Each session is like opening an old book to its first page; it always begins the same."

Sunnie Reynolds

"The beach is deserted, white... and windswept," Sunnie said. In her mind, she watched the scene through a weathered doorway.

"Bright sunlight glints off the water and makes me squint. I turn back to a fire pit where a piece of fish wrapped in a banana palm leaf lays over glowing coals. A strong Gulf breeze blows thru the doorway and cools me; the hot coals flare and the wind carries the smoke up to an opening in the roof."

"Do you know where you are Sunnie?" Dr. Paulding said. He challenged her to enlarge on the scene in her mind, but she stayed silent with eyes closed and concentrated on memories of the previous night's dream.

His gaze remained steady as he silently waited for her to answer, hoping for some sign that she would at last open up and not hold back details. Throughout their sessions over the past few months, he knew Sunnie was suppressing what she had experienced as a child. He patiently put his pen to paper to enter his question then added 'no response' and prepared to try again.

"I was young and alone, how would I know how to cook?" Sunnie asked him sharply and moved her hand over her abdomen.

He didn't answer her question, but added to the notation, 'subject experiencing anxiety and rubbing her stomach'.

"Sandpipers are hunting coquinas along the wave lines," Sunnie said and wiped the palms of her hands on her shirt then reached to ruffle the damp hair away from the back of her neck.

"The porch was built with driftwood and bamboo... all lashed together with vines." She intentionally diverted again. "I usually wake up at this point with stomach cramps."

"Go on Sunnie," Dr. Paulding said. She quieted at his urging and refocused.

"I keep looking at the doorway as if I...expect... something... any second..." She struggled to lie still on the couch and moved her head sharply from left to right then finally sat up, still rubbing her stomach.

Unable to continue, she freed herself from the visions in the dream and opened her eyes wide to the doctor's familiar, book-lined office. Relief flooded over her as the leather sofa squeaked and she shifted position to glance out the window behind her; palm trees, blue skies and daylight brought her back to reality.

"That's all that's left. There's nothing after that." She spat it out as the small store of patience she'd gathered earlier for the session disappeared. Angry with herself for not pushing further, she knew Dr. Paulding expected more. She grabbed a tissue from a nearby dispenser and wiped away the perspiration on the back of her neck and across her forehead then finally looked at him.

"We stop for today." His voice was quiet and calm as he laid his notebook on a side table and focused on her. "Tell me, Sunnie, how do you feel about these memories?" He peered over reading glasses, his graying eyebrows pushed together in concentration.

She wanted to chuckle at the sight, but instead rolled her eyes at the good doctor's textbook question. The answer came to her easily, but wasn't spoken aloud; chronically sleep deprived, frustrated at the lack of progress, and oh yes, ineffective at handling something she didn't remember the details of. Still convinced she could conquer the nightmare by herself, Sunnie did acknowledge Dr. Paulding had been patient with her over the past months and deserved at least a civil answer.

Sunnie faced him, red in the face with what she needed to say. "Angry; I want to remember it all."

She took a deep breath and let it out slowly. "I'm ready to be done with this stupid, meaningless nightmare. There must be more to it, but every time I get close, I wake up! Like, I can't deal with this anymore."

Filled with anger now, she waved her hands to emphasize the last few words. "I want to get on with life and sleep for eight hours like normal people."

Anger surfaced more quickly these days, and so, she gave him what he asked for, something he hadn't heard before.

"I'm afraid." She stopped because she'd never admitted it, not for years, to her mother, to her doctors, never. "I'm afraid the rest of the dream will disappear before I find it," she said in a low whisper and felt her gut quiet. Expecting to see surprise on his face, he smiled at her then quickly baited her with another question.

"Wouldn't that be easier?" he said. She didn't know how to respond.

He tried again. "Do you experience fear at the thought of losing it or of recalling it?"

"I'm... apprehensive... that I'll lose it altogether," she said.

"Why is that?" Dr. Paulding said, animated with enthusiasm. He prepared to hear one of her usual divertive tactics, a sudden off-subject question, Sunnie's method to avoid his probing, but she continued on her own.

"If my mind drops this into the 'recycle bin', I'll never know the why of it or the part of my childhood that's missing. I've adjusted to the lack of sleep... power naps on my lunch hour." She wore a smirk as she waited for Dr. Paulding's reaction to her ill-placed humor. But this time, he didn't react and she realized a door had been opened that couldn't be closed.

"Without the complete dream, how can I fight this?" she said and realized the truth. Silence filled the room.

He cleared his throat and picked up a bottle of water for a sip. "Describe your fears, Sunnie. What scares you the most?"

"It sounds petty." She dropped her head into her hands, tired of the whole charade she'd somehow perpetuated.

"Please," Dr. Paulding coaxed.

"I have phobias about certain things," Sunnie said and looked away to other parts of the office; anything to avoid his eyes. The multi-colored books on shelves around the room were comforting and reminded her of her father's library in their house before the divorce. She looked to the opposite wall and the large abstract by Jackson Pollock. It was a striking tangle of color and movement, one of her favorite ways to divert when a session turned serious.

"Give me an example," he said.

She returned from Pollock's tangle to face Dr. Paulding again.

"I've lived in Florida all my life, but at the mention of 'beach property' I panic." Her voice raised a few decibels at the thought and she breathed deeply to calm down. "I literally can't walk onto a beach."

"What else?" he said.

"I'm apprehensive about traveling to other places. And forget dating, it's impossible to trust anyone new; I don't feel at ease."

She stood up, restless and walked to his now-familiar university diplomas. A bank of six-pane windows partially covered by white louvered Bahama shutters shed their softened light on the wall. She ran her fingers along the frames of his board certifications; child and adolescent Psychiatry and a second in Adult Psychiatry. She lingered at a framed letter from President Kennedy for Dr. Paulding's service in the U.S. Army during the Vietnam War.

"It took over fifteen years of training for those," he said. "But I am most proud of that letter from the President... and most fulfilled."

"I can see why," she said and returned to sit on the sofa again.

"We've discussed how the body adjusts to trauma," Dr. Paulding said and offered her a lemon drop from the dish on the table. "We know something in your youth inflicted a psychological trauma. The body's instinct is to protect you by blocking the details, much the same as it does for a soldier with combat trauma. My job is to help you learn more about the entire event; to realize whatever happened has been over for years...and you're still here in spite of it."

"You make it sound crazy easy," she said. "But I blame myself for not throwing this off and getting on with life." She examined her nails before meeting his eyes again.

"Self-blame will not help." He taps his head. "You have a very competent brain and none of this is your fault. When the memory is unlocked, you'll be able to put it in perspective. As an adult, you'll stop seeing it as a child and more like ancient history that's no longer a threat. Your inner fight or flight mechanism is focused on the unknown right now, Sunnie. When you know the actual event, I'm confident all will readjust." He glanced at his watch, a signal that time was up.

"This was a good session Sunnie and I appreciate your openness. This is a first step and the hardest, so let's keep going forward, shall we? I want you to write down a few keywords from the details you remember before next week's visit. For instance, the doorway you keep glancing through; describe its surroundings, sounds and location; can you do that?"

"Yes, I'll try," Sunnie said. "But it won't be easy." It'll be really hard is what she thought but didn't say.

"It needs to be done, Sunnie." He gave her a serious look. "You'll find it productive, I promise. See you next week and have a lovely weekend. Remember to keep a notepad and pen next to your bed for anything new."

"I will." She answered without enthusiasm.

Outside the office door Sunnie paused to turn her face up to the sun's warmth after an hour of air conditioning. She felt pure freedom when leaving sessions with Dr. Paulding; must be what prisoners feel when granted parole she thought. Except that her freedom would be short-lived and the dream would surely return that night. It was like opening an old book to its first page, it always began the same; she'd begun to doubt the value of their weekly appointments. She walked slowly out the palm-lined sidewalk to the parking lot where her car sat partially shaded.

The late model CRV started easily, she sat idle for a few minutes and waited for the a/c to cool the car before leaving.

Dr. Paulding's statement that she was recalling details as a child started her thinking. Her only memory of being on a real beach was with her mother after the divorce. They'd watched sandpipers scamper bravely up the waterline as waves retreated. Though small in stature and delicate, the little birds bravely scampered in and pushed their beaks deep into the sand. They knew the danger of the oncoming surf as they fed, yet they ran at exactly the right time to avoid the crashing waves.

It suddenly made sense that at age twenty-two she'd been running away and allowing her life to be limited for more than twelve years. She needed to be brave like those little birds and work with Dr. Paulding to uncover the nameless mystery living inside her head.

Feeling encouraged for the first time in a long while, she pulled out of the lot and headed downtown for work at Seashell Realty.

Today, she promised, I'll start today.

Chapter Two – The Decision

Seashell Realty in North Miami sat surrounded on all sides by single-story, flat roof, concrete block buildings. Built up in the prosperous 50's when the area mushroomed with tourists and snow bunnies, the realty building had originally housed a '5 and dime' store. The street had been lined with small mom and pop stores whose owners lived in the modest neighborhoods behind.

Though the area had suffered its ups and downs through economic change, it had again resurfaced as a throwback commercial area. New owners renovated and some even moved into the modest cottages left behind and could walk or ride bikes to work.

There were palm trees and each storefront was shaded by a striped awning, with a decorative planter by the door. Benches along the sidewalk provided ready seating to waiting husbands while their wives shopped. There was a small market, an Italian butcher shop run by a couple from New York, a hardware, a dry cleaner and a cafe specializing in breakfast and lunch 24/7.

Sunnie pulled into the Seashell's hot, uncovered parking lot through the narrow alley. This time of day the space resembled a Tuscan-style oven for cars; the sun beat relentlessly on surrounding concrete, its heat held inside the lot regardless of any breeze outside the space.

She left the cool comfort of her car and dashed to the back door where a wall of cold air greeted her. One of my coworkers must have cranked the A/C up again she thought. Their boss, Walter, had just delivered a lecture to them on saving electricity last week which apparently did not make an impression.

Walter Morgan loved to live green. He didn't mind that the office temperature climbed to seventy-eight degrees by noon in Florida's high humidity months. As long as the electric bill came in below two hundred, he was willing to sweat... when he was in the office.

Sunnie stowed her purse in the bottom desk drawer then stripped off her jacket and hung it over the back of her chair. Their secretary Elsy sat at the front of the office, texting.

"None," Elsy said before Sunnie could ask about messages. "Not a call of any sort. It's as if the entire town has gone on vacation and left us here." She returned to her texting with a lengthy, fire-station-red nail.

"Well, okay, thanks," Sunnie said then walked to the kitchenette for something cold to drink.

After retrieving an iced tea she picked through the day's mail; all of it junk except for a nicely done envelope from a realty company on the west coast.

Inside she found a lucrative invitation to team up on the sale of a property on Decker Island. She turned to the computer and the MLS system for more details and found a picturesque, cracker-style home on two acres of Gulfcoast property.

"Whoa, we're talking quite a commission on this one, even shared with the company agent... a Mrs. Quinones," Sunnie said.

Elsy looked up from her phone as Sunnie squinted to read the name at the bottom of the letter. "You could wear those glasses you keep in your purse," she said, never losing a beat on her cell; one of the reasons Seashell kept her was her uncanny ability to multi-task and stay accurate in her work.

"Where's the fun in that?" Sunnie said. "This way it's a challenge. Where's Walter?"

"He walked down to the Café to get some lunch," Elsy said.

Sunnie grabbed the letter and put it back in its envelope. "I'm going down there, be back soon."

"Don't worry, I'll hold down the overwhelming business going on here," Elsy said.

The Short Stop Café was the only eatery in the borough and the neighborhood gathering spot. Sunnie walked rather than drive after her morning on the couch and soon reached the Café's hot pink façade, much hotter under the noon sun. She gratefully pulled the door open to step inside.

One of the waitresses waved to her then poured coffee for a customer. "Be with you in a second," she said.

Sunnie looked around, it was packed as usual; she recognized several people who worked nearby. With booths around its perimeter and chrome-legged tables in the center, the place was a step back to the 50's and 60's. She could see why Walter liked it here she thought and looked to the back of the room.

Walter sat at 'his table', laptop open, papers stacked around it, his cell phone at hand. Sunnie knew he thought of this as his satellite office and frequently sent documents to print in the office, while smoozing with friends who stopped by. Of course the A/C is cold here, but that couldn't be a factor she thought with a wry smile.

She'd grown close to Walter and his wife Ellie over the years and appreciated their friendship, so as she drew nearer and saw the large corned beef on rye he was putting away, she just had to mention it.

"What do you think you're doing?" Sunnie said and sat down in front of him. He visibly jumped then glared at her.

"Guess you didn't see me coming eh?" she said, stating the obvious. "You know you're not supposed to be eating that stuff."

"You're not going to tell, are you?" he asked in a muffled voice as he finished the bite.

"Only if it happens again, Ell gets too upset." After a mild heart attack last year, his wife made it her mission to enforce his cardiac diet plan and gave Sunnie full latitude to help.

"What're you doing here anyway?" he asked, a little harsh, though more relaxed now that his eating transgression would remain in confidence, this time.

Sunnie put the letter in front of him and waited for his reaction while she took a look around the room. Several people waved to her from their red-checkered tables. She'd been with Shell Realty four years now; surprising how many people she'd met here in 'Walter's 'office'.

"Wow." He remarked with a modicum of reserve. "Why would they share a commission like this?"

"I can only guess they've had trouble unloading it." Sunnie said. "And we're in the greater Miami area – you know, movie stars, models, socialites. I say we can't look a gift horse in the mouth."

"What exactly does that mean?" He wiped some hot mustard from the corner of his mouth. "I've never understood completely; another of your grandmother's favorites I assume?"

"Yes, it is. It means realty companies who haven't had a decent sale in six months, much less one that involves a quarter-million commission, should not question it." She reached for the pickle on his plate, "You gonna eat this?"

"You're right, of course; you want to take it on?" he said and offered her the pickle.

"You mean it?" Sunnie said.

He nodded, but stifled a smile. "You've worked hard holding us together through this recession with your gift for finding customers. You deserve this one, Sunnie."

"Walter, I won't let you down," she said and came around the table to drop a peck on his red cheek.

"Okay, okay, don't go maudlin on me," he protested. "Ellie might hear gossip based on what people see in here and I'm in no shape to lose her."

"Like, she would walk out on you!" Sunnie said. "How long has it been…thirty-some years?"

"Thirty-six to be exact and I look forward to many more. Alright, let's go back to the office and formulate a plan for your trip over there. I wanna take a look at the company and be sure they're on the level." He jammed all his papers into a briefcase and Sunnie picked up his laptop.

"I'll talk to the owner before you leave," Walter said from several paces in front of her.

Still stuck on the 'before you take a trip over there' part, Sunnie followed him out of the Café and tried to act like it was no biggy.

On the walk back, the reasons why she couldn't do it materialized one by one. The fear of the unfamiliar roiled inside her and sent a litany of SOS's through her brain. You don't ordinarily leave home base for another city; the water surrounding the island will be limiting and scary; you have to get quality rest and need a good mattress in familiar surroundings.

This is like a trip to the dentist, she thought, necessary and scary at the same time. Actually, she'd prefer the dentist to the trip.

Chapter Three - Road Trip

Two days later Sunnie drove south to Alligator Alley and west to Fort Myers. She'd used two days as a buffer in making the final decision to go and even asked Dr. Paulding's opinion. It was with his encouragement that she found the strength to say 'yes' to the trip.

Her mother's face had washed white when Sunnie told her.

"Well, that is news," Maggie had said. "Come in out of the heat." Sunnie followed her inside the small mid-century modern house.

It was not the house she was first raised in and it had never felt like home. Maggie bought it after she and dad separated. It was one of many developed somewhere in the 50's. Her mother still socialized with a few neighbors who stayed on after their kids left. Others sold out to developers who tore down the older homes and built single-story cement block homes of stucco and glass.

"How did this trip come about?" Maggie had asked. Sunnie detected the caution in her mother's voice; it was always there when Sunnie attempted to do something out of the ordinary. It was aggravating that at her age, her mother still felt the need to protect her from what she might not be capable of. Perhaps Maggie's inference was unintended and out of love Sunnie thought; she had done it since the divorce, but it was no less hard to tolerate.

Sunnie's father lived across town with his second wife and family; she rarely saw him except on holidays. She loved him as she did Maggie, but it was easier to stay aloof after the split between the two.

"I'm so glad you're getting out, dear," Maggie had finally said.

"Well, it's time, don't you think, Mom?" Sunnie had tried to act confident and hoped it translated that way, but her mother continued to study her face as she spoke.

"Why of course; we all need a little variety in life, don't we?" Maggie had said. "How about some coffee; I just made a fresh pot?"

"I really can't, Mom; I have a million things to do before leaving in the morning." Disappointment brushed across her mother's face then disappeared.

"That's understandable, dear," Maggie had said. "Now you must call me if you need anything, a piece of luggage? How about snacks for the trip?" They'd walked together to the door.

"No mom, I'm all set, but thanks." They embraced and her mother let her go quickly.

"Good luck with the house sale dear and be safe."

Sunnie looked down at the front seat to retrieve a bag of munchies and a canned juice drink from the cooler. The drive across Alligator Alley was a little boring; she'd heard descriptions of it from her father in the past and rejoiced in the fact that so far, no twelve-foot alligators were relaxing in the roadway and no swarms of locust were plastered on her car's windshield.

She smiled as she thought of earlier days when dad and mom were still together. He'd once encountered a huge cloud of locusts and his car, a beautiful Bellaire, was covered with hard-shelled, multi colored insect bodies. Each measured about three inches in length and stuck where they'd hit. He literally scraped with soap and water for hours before the family auto was clean again.

Sunnie had so far evaded her anxieties by concentrating on other things; like mentally packing her suitcase and making sure she had enough clothing for a couple days' stay. She didn't understand why the initial assessment of the property wasn't done by Island Realty, but remained grateful for their generous offer which made up for doing all their paperwork.

I can do this she told herself and for the moment, the voice inside saying she couldn't was silent and she concentrated on the road ahead.

The house was described as late eighteenth century, built by one of the first inhabitants on Decker Island. She was excited to explore it and hoped someone hadn't mucked around with it too much. 'Redecorate' seemed to be the mantra of any contemporary who dabbled in real estate these days. 'Let's modernize and flip it' they say. She hated what she'd seen in some flips; original fixtures ripped out, period kitchen equipment replaced with stainless steel farm sinks and handcrafted woodwork thrown in a dumpster.

More recently, inside walls were being removed to make 'open concept' homes. Everyone gets to hear and experience each other in one room along with the noise coming out of the kitchen - yuck. Sunnie believed that's what tenement dwellers experienced in the turn of the century and no one was waxing sentimental on those good old days.

Off the bridge exit, she pulled into Island Realty's parking lot, turned off the ignition and exhaled. Taking time to collect herself, one glance in the mirror told her, that thanks to the humidity, the hair she straightened that morning was back to a poor impression of orphan Annie. She quickly tucked some stray strands behind her ears, put on some lip gloss and opened the car door.

The realty building was Spanish-influenced and painted pink. What a surprise she thought wryly, coming as she did from Miami, the leader in pink buildings. It was surrounded by suitable greenery; palms, aloe plants and Spanish bayonet under the windows. Very few break-ins to this building she imagined as she eyed the plants' sharp points on her way to the entrance. A middle-aged, very attractive woman greeted her and held the door open.

"You must be Sunnie Reynolds," the woman said and shook Sunnie's hand as she stepped inside.

"Millie Hannigan?" Sunnie said.

"Yes, I'm so glad you decided to come in today. I'm going away up north to New Hampshire for a week and hoped to talk with you beforehand. Did you have a good drive from Miami, Sunnie?"

"Yes, very nice, beautiful day for it." Sunnie smiled and took the proffered chair in front of Millie, who rushed around her desk and immediately opened a file folder.

"Good! Now, let me fill you in...but before that, here are the front and back door keys." She reached over the desk and dropped a wad of older keys in Sunnie's hand.

"That one is for the generator, which currently isn't working. Yes, that's right, but there is garbage pickup..." Millie rolled her eyes upward and paused to take a breath.

Well, what a relief Sunnie thought, her mind already going sour grapes on the whole electrical thing.

Milly ran on; "There are kerosene lamps in all the rooms and plenty of reserve fuel, I made sure of...."

"Whoa there Millie, just a moment," Sunnie said. "Are you telling me there'll be no A/C, not even lights or a fan?"

"Well, as of yesterday, yes," she said straight-faced.

Sunnie began to gather her bag, indicating she would be leaving, but Millie stood up and wrung her hands.

"I have someone working on the generator today and it should be up and running by the time you get there."

Sunnie hesitated; I must be crazy she thought but sat back down for any more good news Millie might offer.

"There's a wood stove and I had 'Steve' pile plenty of kindling outside the kitchen door for you, enough for the few days you'll be here. Do you have an ice chest?" Before Sunnie had time to answer, Millie added, "If not, I have a large ice chest here if you'd like to borrow it."

"I brought my own, but I will take the extra, sounds like I'm going to need it; groceries?" Sunnie asked skeptically.

"Yes, the Island Market is just down the street." Millie arose and approached the map on the wall.

"Now let me show you where the property is located..."

"You're not coming with me?" Sunnie asked in disbelief.

"Well, I guess I could, though it really shouldn't be necessary. If you'd like me to...." Millie's voice trailed off while she looked down at her desk and rearranged papers.

"No, that's fine, I'm sure I can figure it out from this map." After all, Sunnie thought, it is an island, how bad could it be. "I'm assuming there are sheets on the bed, dishes, and basic necessities? Is there a water supply?" she said as a joke.

"That's another thing…" Millie quickly replied.

"What?" It was the only word Sunnie could safely say and remain courteous.

"A well pump is near the kitchen door, but it's rather smelly, rotten eggs, Sulphur water you know," Millie said. "The cistern for rain water catch is quite full which gives you an indoor shower and water to the sinks as long as the supply holds out. It's treated and quite safe, but you might pick up some bottled water at the grocery for drinking."

Sunnie called Walter afterwards so he wouldn't worry and filled him in on the description Millie supplied. His only words, "You're only there for two days – how bad can it be?"

"Thanks Walter," she said and hung up the phone. Something told her Walter knew all along about the house's condition and didn't want to come over himself.

The route to the listing was simple and Sunnie drove the two rut lane through palms and underbrush to the front porch just as the sun dipped beneath the horizon. She sat looking at the old house for a few minutes; could be in northern Florida, Alabama or Louisiana and fit right in. Lots of bleached-out siding peeked through an old coat of blue paint; she noted that the windows and doors were intact, a comfort since she'd be alone that night. Trepidation ramped up at the thought, but she fought it down and reached for her purse.

She climbed the steps dragging her suitcase behind and set it aside to pull open one of the wooden screen doors. She peered through the beveled glass of the double front doors. Everything was dark inside and she consciously put down her phobia of new places to insert one of Millies' keys into the brass-plated latch cover.

The door swung open easily with a few squeaks and didn't fall off its frame, a good sign. The air smelled stale as she slowly entered the dusky hallway. Spiders and rats were her worst fear in old houses although the surprise of a sleeping vagrant in Miami stayed right up there on her chart, too.

A kerosene parlor lamp sat to her right on the entryway table and she put down her purse to pick up a butane-lighter left beside it. No ordinary lamp, it was large and fashioned of brass with a fancy white, opaque-glass shade. Its light filled most of the hallway and the front parlor to the right, enabling her to take in the somber old room. A picture on the mantel caught her interest, a young soldier in uniform, perhaps vintage WWII era, stared back at her. She couldn't help wondering if he lived to return to the Island.

She walked slowly down the long hallway towards the back of the house and lit two more kerosene lamps as she found them. With each step her stress level unconsciously heightened until she squeezed the purse under her arm so hard that the menu button on her cell phone emitted a loud BEEP! She jerked, but recovered the purse.

Shaky and relieved at the same time, she realized nothing was out of the ordinary so far and exhaled normally for the first time since entering the hallway.

In past experiences with dark old houses in Miami and, in view of all her existing fears, it would have been much easier had someone come along with her. She'd learned it was better to know up front if people or animals occupied a place and be ready to run. She supposed with some envy, and a little irritation, that Millie was already at the airport.

Peering into the dim light at the end of the hall, she could just make out the edge of a table, perhaps in a kitchen. She rallied and continued toward it, opening the remaining doors down the hallway.

She found a large library on the left and being one of her favorite things in the world, she couldn't resist peeking at a few of the shelves before moving on. A huge oak desk and a comfy-looking overstuffed chair sat near the double window, just the sort of place she'd love to spend time in.

Intrigued, she skimmed across the books on the nearest shelf and found classics by Homer, Aristotle and early Greek mythology. On the shelf above, authors from the thirties and forties, Albert Camus, The Stranger and The Pearl by John Steinbeck, so many she could pull off the shelves and enjoy. But she needed to get an early start in the morning and resolved to visit in the light of day. Whoever lived there apparently spent a lot of time collecting and reading.

She chose the last bedroom on the back corner of the house with the biggest bed and left her bag and computer there. Furnishings were noted so far to be of good quality and original to the place which made her thankful that antique raiders hadn't foraged the property.

After three trips to and from the car, she hoisted the ice chest onto the big oak table in the kitchen and breathed a sigh of relief. Her back and hands ached; should have known better than to lug all that stuff in at once she thought. Knowing she was alone was a relief, but she had the rest of the night to be alone and the tightness in her stomach stirred at the thought. She sat down in one of the wooden kitchen chairs and rubbed her forehead, elbows on the table.

Upon looking up, a huge, vintage wood stove 'stared' back at her from across the table. It was a monster-sized piece of cast iron with fancy brass inlays on its two warming compartments and double oven doors. The firebox in the center had been cleaned out, its door left open and ready for a new fire to be laid.

Given her current state of mind, the stove reminded her of an animation in a Disney movie; eyes - the brass inlays; its mouth, the fire box, and wide open.

"Okay," she said to no one in particular and arose from the chair, deciding a cold supper of lunch meat and canned peaches made more sense at that hour. Besides, she didn't want to bring in fire kindling that might house lizards and spiders.

After the 'feast' she returned to the bedroom to discover that the windows were fitted with screens and their sashes opened easily. A nice cross-breeze stirred through the room and the night's sultry heat began to be bearable. "Hope it continues through the night," Sunnie whispered, knowing that tropical breezes frequently disappeared around 3 a.m.

After night time meds, she turned back the bedcovers and found the sheets fresh with no musty smell. Hallelujah! "Thanks Millie." She stripped to underwear and crawled into bed after a very long day.

Sometime in the middle of the night, the nightmare found Sunnie and she again looked out over an ocean... somewhere. Remembering her vow to try harder, she decided to attempt control of the dream and see everything she could.

She turned to the inside of the room where the fire pit glowed and its smoke rose to the open vent hole in the roof. She looked back at the door and a raggedy-edged dark shadow suddenly broke the flow of sunlight entering the doorway. She jumped awake, wet with sweat.

Not sure where she was, she grabbed her phone off the bedside table and turned on its flashlight app. The earlier breeze had stopped as predicted and humidity hung in the night air.

Oriented, she threw off the sheets and walked to the bathroom. A cold washcloth cooled her neck and after a drink of water, she wrote down what she'd seen for Dr. Paulding then returned to bed.

Chapter Four – Good Morning

Near dawn, in that familiar, half-awake stage when sound begins to seep into one's consciousness, Sunnie felt the coolness of the hour before sunrise and turned over to get comfy again. A car door slammed outside and she jumped up to yank on her robe.

Down the hallway, she could just make out a man dressed in denim as he banged on the old screen then saw her approaching. She peeked out the glass of the front doors at him.

"Morning, I'm Steve Evans." His smile was entirely too bright for the time of morning. She'd glanced at the parlor clock in passing; six a.m. indeed, she hadn't seen that hour of the day in years.

"I work for Millie at the realty office." He looked again through the screen door. "You must be Sunnie Reynolds; Millie said you'd be here."

"Yes Mr. Evans, what can I do for you?" She wrapped her robe tighter and tied the sash.

"Millie asked me to show you the generator, stoke the stove and generally show you around." He paused for a moment and she found herself looking at him and wondering if she should let him in. People get murdered all the time after letting strangers in. Then she remembered Millie talking about her handyman 'Steve'.

"May I come in?" he asked cautiously. It dawned on her; he's waiting for an answer.

"Yes, of course, please do." She unlatched the door. "Sorry, I'm half asleep and rather dull-witted at this hour."

"No problem, I know it's early." He smiled again. "I just don't have the luxury since my job starts at dawn on a daily basis."

"Would you like some coffee?" she asked, then remembered there was no electricity and rephrased the question. "I mean, would you like to show me how to 'stoke' the stove so that I can make you some coffee?"

"Tell you what," he said, "I'll just go start the generator then you can use the microwave." He winked at her and she remembered something; cute, my dad used to do that.

"I didn't know I had one," Sunnie said, referring to the microwave.

"Millie left it with me," Steve said. His blue eyes looked straight into hers and she suddenly felt very uncomfortable standing there in her underwear and robe.

"I'll just meet you in the kitchen in a few minutes Mr. Evans." She left him standing there, assuming he knew where the kitchen was.

"Please, call me Steve, everyone does." He called out as she withdrew to the bedroom to throw on some jeans and a shirt.

She joined him in the kitchen and they walked out to an old wooden shed with structural sag on one side. Steve swung open the double doors and they stood in front of the large gasoline engine inside. He explained the generator's operation until Sunnie felt confident enough to start it by herself.

"This is all new for me," she said and tried to do it exactly as he told her. The noisy engine fired up on her first try.

"Wow, it started." She actually did a little jump of joy - not her usual behavior.

Steve grinned at her. "You did good Sunnie."

She grinned back. "Thank-you, how about that cup of coffee I offered earlier?"

They sat on the front porch swing with microwave instant coffees, the early morning air still cool enough to be comfortable.

"How long have you lived here?" Sunnie said.

"We moved from the east coast in 1997 when I was twelve to take care of my grandfather as he got older," Steve said. "My parents liked it and wanted me in a smaller school setting anyway. We'd moved a lot with dad in the military and it didn't take us long to love this island."

Sunnie watched the squirrels run and chatter at each other in the trees while he talked. A family of six ibis decided to take a stroll from the brush edging the yard and poked their curved beaks into the sandy soil for snails and frogs.

"I don't know if you realize it, but this is my grandfather's house."

Steve's remark pulled her back to his blue eyes.

"No, I didn't; is that his picture on the mantel?" she said.

"Yes, that's him just before he left for the Great War."

"Then wouldn't you rather keep the house in your family than sell it?" she said.

"I have my memories of him and a few mementos of our earlier times together. What about you, Sunnie; have you always lived in Florida?" Steve said.

"Yes, mostly in northern Miami. After the divorce, mom and I moved to another burb. I think it was so she wouldn't have to run into dad's new wife in the same circles."

"I'm sorry; that must have been hard on you." He cast a sympathetic look her way.

"A little, but not as much as you'd think; they managed to be good parents despite it all."

"How did you wind up in real estate?" Steve said.

"I was one of those kids without a plan after high school and extremely shy. I thought four more years of school would be gruesome." Sunnie left out the nightmare; only her parents and Dr. Paulding knew about it.

"I looked at other options and hit upon the real estate thing. The older homes in Miami were intriguing and the thought of matching up the right buyer with the right house for a living appealed to me. What about you; is this your 'dream' job?" Sunnie said.

"Dream job? No." He laughed, "I left the island and went on to four years of college."

"Really? What was your major?" She said.

"I graduated with a master's in fine art; I'm an artist when I'm not working my day job."

"Wait, 'the' Steve Evans of Florida Waters?" Sunnie said.

"Yes, you may have seen the Gallery coming onto the island?" He flushed as he acknowledged his accomplishment.

"I did," she said. "I'd love to see your work; maybe later I'll stop in."

"I belong to Island Realty today," he said. "But for you, just call and let me know when you'd like a tour; it's the off season, so viewing is by special request."

"I will," she said.

"And now, as pleasant as this is, a leaky sink is calling my name on the other side of the island." He joked, "And I must go."

"I need to get busy, too. Nice meeting you Steve. I have to admit I was a little skeptical last night with no A/C, but the place does seem to grow on a person."

"The island is like that and it's why I'm here to stay." He paused at the edge of the porch. "Don't forget to call me when you'd like to see the Gallery."

"I will," she said and watched as he drove off in a run-down white pickup truck with Island Realty's logo on the side. Interesting, he's a college grad and satisfied to stay on an island, paint and do plumbing for a living.

She returned inside to begin inventory of the house.

Sunnie knew that settlers in the mid 1800's commonly built with cypress and native yellow pine transported by boat from the mainland. She'd seen a few Cracker houses in her career, but this one was different; it had post and beam 'bones' versus the more common timber frame style and sat firmly on a coral rock foundation. The eaves were built especially deep, obvious assets for keeping both shutters and window casements in good shape from heavy downpours during tropical storms. She hoped the original pine, now hard as iron, would pass termite inspection with flying colors.

More amazing was the original interior woodwork, wallpapers and period furnishings retained through the years. To some, it could be a detriment, but to buyers interested in the home's historical worth, they'd be a major selling point. She finished the inventory, took pictures of each room and began to enter all to her laptop.

The vintage claw-foot tub, octagonal floor tiles and six-pane windows made the high-ceilinged bathroom her favorite room, after the library, of course. She vowed to spend time in that tub before leaving.

After several hours, her eyes burned from staring at the computer's screen and she took a break to look out the window and do some stretch-outs against its wide sill. Walter may know the name of a good book appraiser she thought, still in work mode. It seemed odd that the house would be sold with all its furnishings and she wondered why Steve wasn't interested in keeping it.

As she watched out the window, seagulls crossed the deep blue sky toward the shoreline. A new thought came to mind, one that she'd never entertained at home. If she had the courage, the beach would probably be beautiful.

She felt stronger since the previous night alone then at any time in her life and pushing beyond her comfort zone would be good for her; Dr. Paulding had said.

Perhaps it takes little steps she thought, begin gradually, maybe take a walk and get some pictures to send back to Walter. She bargained with her fear and declared that if she reached the beachfront, she'd keep walking as far as she could.

The tidal basins would be alive with salt mosquitos this time of year and there were several marshes on the island according to the map in Millie's office. Sunnie's white skin gleaming in the sun would be quite a target she thought. It amazed her that she could find humor in the moment even as the old fears festered inside and threatened to make her reverse her decision to go.

She changed to long pants and slathered on mosquito repellant. Just thinking about approaching the beach ran niggling tension up her spine, but she was determined and took a deep, shaky breath then let it out slowly. Maggie always told her 'Walk it off' when anxiety flared; easy for her to say, Sunnie thought, but she meant well.

Outside, the beach path began at the edge of the backyard. Sunnie grabbed her camera from the kitchen counter then faced off in the path's direction. "Small steps," she said aloud and started with one then another out the back door and down the worn, wooden stoop.

A sandy pathway led into the tropical green growth of sea grape, cottonwoods and mangroves. A breeze from the water swept through the gum trees above in a soft whisper and cooled her.

She stopped to look back, the house was out of sight and she was surrounded by island jungle, undisturbed for many years. Palms leaned away from the shore, some were coconut palms and some were palmettos grown just as tall. Vines and smaller plants she didn't recognize made the undergrowth thick as the Pollock painting on Dr. Paulding's wall; how similar they were she thought.

Did she hear someone following? Don't be silly she berated herself, there's no one here to follow me. She shivered and pushed herself to continue forward. Self-coaching didn't fully set her straight though and she wanted to go back.

"Okay, enough," she said aloud and bent to focus on two green anole lizards crossing the path. They stopped to look around then scurried away, their tails high, spooked by her intrusion. She used to play with anoles as a child and put them on a sheet of colored paper to make them change their color from bright lime green to dark brown. If the paper's color was outside their ability, they turned a mottled shade. Maybe that's what I'm doing now she thought, trying to change to a color beyond my ability.

What if I'm not brave enough? Sunnie forced herself to look ahead and started walking again. The path ended more suddenly than she expected where the sandy edge of the beach began. She dared not look beyond the sand, but by common sense she knew the aqua-blue of the Gulf lay only a few yards away.

The offshore breeze cooled her perspiration and a clash of mixed feelings hit her. Familiar anxieties lodged deep inside made her slow her pace.

Her mother used to hold her hand as they waded together into the water carefree and playful. Since the nightmare she hadn't…couldn't do it, but she wanted to put her feet into the water again. She looked down to the sand in front of her…one step then another.

She willed herself to move the last few steps to the water's edge and leaned over to swish the tepid seawater with her fingers. Two small, yellow-striped fish swam and dodged around her hand and she watched them with delight as they darted for the coral rock nearby.

A stone crab surprised her then tucked himself into a shallow hole convinced that he was invisible. "I can identify fella," she said. "I want to turn and run to the safety of the house."

With a deep breath of the ocean's familiar smell, she straightened up to look at the deserted shoreline; it wouldn't be this pristine in Miami. White powder sand led to the tropical aqua water of the Gulf. Gulls flew overhead, diving at will into the water for minnows. Sandpipers ran together down the shore.

She took one last look before turning on impulse to walk back for the swimsuit she'd packed and never thought she'd use. Is this me or some newly-arrived alien, she mused.

Halfway to the path, she noticed a rundown shack off to her left, mostly covered by brush. Full of newfound courage, she decided to explore it and walked toward it. She took a picture of it then turned to the water and snapped several of the sea gulls circling overhead. After checking the settings on her camera she turned again to the shack.

As she drew closer, her steps slowed... something strange about the old place...

Peripheral vision closed down suddenly as only the pieces of driftwood, bamboo and palm leaves on the porch roof were visible through the undergrowth at the edge of the jungle. A familiar knot punched the pit of her stomach and she was frozen to one spot on the sand.

In a few seconds she was awash in reality mixed with nightmare and completely overshadowed by an unknown fear.

I've crossed over to the dream she thought... and I'm powerless to understand where I am.

She moved backwards like some crazy funhouse movie character; in her haste she fell over a rock, but jumped back up.

Then she was running the path back to the house, unaware of when she started to run.

Her lungs burned, she had no thought of stopping. It can't be; the words kept repeating in her head. It was exactly like the place in her dream...but how?

Sunnie reached the yard gasping for air and pushed through the back door to collapse at the kitchen table. Her heart threatened to pound out of her chest and she struggled to calm down. She repeated over and over, there's no such place...it's just a dream....

But she knew that porch with its strange roof; though aged and rundown she'd seen it hundreds of times before in her nightmare.

Her brain couldn't get a grip on the concept so she coached herself to concentrate on the real world, the kitchen she sat in, the big old iron cook stove, the hand pump at the sink.

Gradually her heart began to slow; she pulled a bottle of water from the ice chest to hold against her throbbing head then took a drink. Its icy cold plunged down her parched throat and strengthened her sense of reality.

She took a couple of acetaminophen tabs and lay down on the bed. The headache was a doozy, triggered by the nightmare that was now a 'daymare'. She managed to drift off to sleep for a while and awakened with a start to discover she was on top of the white coverlet, boots, jeans and all.

Sunnie wondered if she'd actually dreamed the entire thing. Maybe it isn't the same place she tried to reason, but she knew it was. The place in her nightmare was now a reality.

Chapter Five - Sharing

Sunnie spent two hours soul-searching the morning's experience and teetered on the edge of losing herself entirely. It would have been so easy to give in to all the fear and confusion; to continue with therapy for the rest of her life, perhaps never to discover the real truth and why this happened; never to walk on a beach again...so easy.

But she remembered something Dr. Paulding said during the last visit and it brought her back; 'You have a competent brain Sunnie...when the memory is unlocked, you'll put it in perspective...and stop seeing it through child's eyes'. Was today's discovery her wake-up call, a step toward opening the locked-up story in her brain?

She decided to call Dr. Paulding, knowing he'd be able to guide her. The receptionist answered.

"This is Sunnie Reynolds, is the doctor in, please?" After a few minutes she heard his voice.

"Hello Sunnie, what can I do for you?"

"I'm on Decker Island as we discussed. I had a... distressing experience this morning."

"What is it Sunnie... are you alright?" he said.

"It's difficult to describe... I've found the location in my dream." It felt good to say it, but scary at the same time.

"I don't understand," he said. "The place in your nightmare really exists?"

"Yes, it does and it's right here on this island." She told him about her experience and how his words gave her courage to approach the beach.

"Sunnie, I'm... speechless," he said. "You've made wonderful progress and I'm very proud of you for launching out the way you have. I'm a little worried that in your haste you may have chosen a place most like your dream in an effort to make it real."

"What are you saying; that I'm crazy enough to do such a thing...?" She felt the old anger rise inside her.

"No, no Sunnie, that's not what I mean at all. You're not crazy. I'm just cautioning that because you want so badly to find your way out...your mind might have made it easier to accept your discovery as the one in your dream."

"Go on," she said.

"I'm asking that you proceed now based on fact, Sunnie. There's a possibility it's the real location, but research it as you would a property; confirm its history and connection to you. Will you do that?"

"I see your point and I will," Sunnie said, but she was awash with excitement and fear. He'd appealed to her exacting nature and clearly, she had to be correct in her identification of the shack and prove a legitimate connection to the place.

She called Elsy next.

"Elsy, it's Sunnie."

"Sunnie, it's good to hear from you. So how's it going? Must be tough being stranded on a tropical island to work, huh?"

She doesn't know how tough Sunnie thought. "Yes, it's really tough – ha ha. Listen, can you do me a favor and look up any beachfront building permits for structures in the vicinity of the house here? Look back through the 50's if you can and let me know what you find."

"Of course, for you, anything, you know that," Elsy said. "Besides, it's still dead around here and I'm desperate for something to do. I'll send you an email by tomorrow, okay?"

"Beautiful, thank-you so much, Elsy."

Thinking more logically, Sunnie changed to Bermuda shorts and sandals then grabbed her car keys to drive over to Island Realty.

Steve's lived here all his life, she thought; maybe he can tell me more about the shack. She didn't' want to pull him away from his work, but she was driven to find out more at this point, and far from being sensitive to anyone's needs but her own.

"Steve's out on the island taking care of properties." Millie's secretary said. "I can send him over when he checks back in, probably by four o'clock or so." She studied Sunnie's face.

"Thanks, I'd appreciate that," Sunnie said and silently hoped the secretary hadn't noticed her unkempt hair and wrinkled shirt; from the secretary's critical expression though, the wish was wasted.

Sunnie managed to pick up some ice for the coolers and a few groceries at the Island Store before driving back to the house.

Preparing supper in case Steve stayed to eat seemed a good idea since it also served as occupational therapy for her anxiety level.

He knocked on the screen door around four-thirty and Sunnie jumped at the sound.

"Come in, please," she said as calmly as possible. "I have supper ready; would you like to join me? There're some questions I need answers to." She blurted it all out with little finesse and he hesitated.

"...Unless you have other responsibilities?" Sunnie said. "My goodness, I'm sorry. I am so thoughtless sometimes."

"No, it's nothing like that." He looked at her for a few seconds and sensed a difference in her demeanor. "Are you alright, Sunnie?"

She tried to laugh at his question. "I'm okay, I had, ah... an unusual...experience this morning and thought you might be able to help, someone I could talk to...that's all. If it isn't a convenient time, I certainly understand." She put on a reassuring smile and hoped it was believable.

"I appreciate the offer," Steve said. "I've been working outside in the sun all day. Supper sounds good, if I could just wash up before we sit down?"

"Of course, help yourself to the bathroom; there're towels and washcloths in the cabinet, but you already know that don't you?" Her face grew warm with embarrassment. "You're welcome to shower as long as the cistern holds out." She joked, but hoped it actually would.

Steve returned to the kitchen later, smelling of soap, his wet hair combed back. He was lightly sunburned and wore a clean shirt retrieved from his truck.

"This looks good." He surveyed the table where she'd laid out a large salad and some fish tacos.

"Thank-you; please, sit down and help yourself. Would you like some iced tea?" Sunnie said.

"I usually spend the evening with a gallon of tea after a hot day like this." He poured for them both then took a deep draught from his glass. "This is my favorite brand; let me guess, the Island Market." His blue eyes sparkle.

"You got it, the only store in town." She relaxed a little. "How do you keep going when it's ninety-three degrees and the humidity's the same?"

"I'm used to it, raised here, mostly ignore it I guess. How about you, Sunnie; are you hot-weather adapted or an A/C person?"

"When the temp goes over eighty-five, I'm inside, except for early morning or evening," she said.

They began to eat and after a while Sunnie decided to give him the morning's story straight on. He probably wouldn't believe her and might think her crazy, but she hoped not. She needed answers and didn't have time to be subtle since she was leaving tomorrow. She felt comfortable with him which was a rarity, so she put down her fork and began.

"Steve, do you believe dreams can become reality? I mean, have you ever dreamed something and found a real place similar to what you dreamed about?" she said.

"I have to say yes, I do believe in dreams and the occasional Deja vu experience. I think everyone has had at least one. Why do you ask?" he said.

She took a breath and plunged in. "I've had the same nightmare over and over since I was ten. There's a beach shack beside the ocean with a porch of driftwood pieces and bamboo. There's a fire pit inside and I'm cooking a fish."

"Go on," he said.

"I've been in and out of psych rehab for years because of sleep deprivation and other things I won't go into now." Sunnie wondered how he felt about the woman across the table now that he'd heard she's a basket case.

"Is it the hut on the beach behind the house?" he said.

"I think so, wait... you know it?" she said and straightened to listen to his reply. Up to that moment, it was part of a crazy dream sequence in a bad horror movie, hers alone.

He gazed past her for a moment.

"Yes I do, I used to play there as a kid," he said.

"How long has it been there and who built it?" Sunnie said quickly.

"I don't know who originally built it. What else do you remember Sunnie?" he said.

"Well, that's all, the rest is a blank." She lied and intentionally left out the fear.

"But you think there's more?" he said.

"Yes, I know there is, but my doctor says my mind is in protective mode. I...had a bad time of it earlier today when I discovered the place, an anxiety attack pure and frightening. It's taken time to get a grip again." Her voice shook a little as she said it.

He got up to extend his hand and she reached for it. "I'm sorry to hear that," he said and pulled her gently from the chair.

"You know the only way to conquer a fear is to face it head-on, don't you?" He looked into her eyes. "I'd be honored to be a friend if you need one and help in any way I can."

Maybe a friend is what I need she thought. It was easy to step into his arms and rest against his shoulder for a few moments. Tears came as she related what she knew of her dream.

She pulled away then to look at him. "I just want you to know, I never do this, Steve."

"You don't strike me as the clinging vine type, if that's what you're getting at," he said.

"And please don't have any unrealistic idea about what this means, either," she said.

"No ideas, Sunnie," he said in reassurance and handed her a napkin to dry her tears. He sat down and looked at her.

"Come on, let's finish these delicious tacos and you can tell me all about your real estate career," Steve said.

"Not much to tell. I've been licensed since high school and make a comfortable living with Seashell Realty." It was enough to turn the conversation away from her mentality to more mundane subjects and they relaxed through the rest of the meal.

"Supper was delicious Sunnie, thank-you." Steve said as he prepared to leave.

"I'm glad you enjoyed it and that you put up with my outburst earlier," she said.

He hesitated to open the door and turned back to her.

"What if we take a walk to that old hut together and see what it brings?" he said.

She felt it might be possible to return with him by her side, but it was too soon. "I can't go back yet," she said. "It's taken too much out of me." Just the idea of returning caused her panic to stir.

"Yes, of course, I understand," Steve said. "Then how about dinner tomorrow afternoon about four – my treat?"

He pushed through the screen door. "Give me a chance to pay back tonight's supper?"

"You don't have to do that," she said.

He leaned over and put a kiss on her cheek. "Tomorrow at four?"

"Okay," she said, but thought *great, now he feels sorry for me.*

The next day while waiting on Steve to arrive, Sunnie reached to a high shelf in the library to pull down Alice in Wonderland and noticed another, much newer book beside it, 'Alice's Adventures Underground'. It was a facsimile released in 1964 of Lewis Carroll's original manuscript for 'Alice'. She hadn't known it even existed and browsed through it as she sat in the library's overstuffed chair.

It occurred to her she was on a similar path to Alice's as she experienced bizarre changes in her life. Sunnie knew she must find her way out of her 'rabbit hole' nightmare and understand all of the hut's implications.

Steve's knock at the front door brought her back to reality. Almost sorry to leave the library's cozy chair, she glanced up the hallway. Seeing him there in jeans and dark blue t-shirt seemed a good enough reason and she put the book aside.

"Hi," she said. For some reason they hugged each other as if it had been years.

"Wow, is this how you greet all your handymen?" he said.

"Nope, just this one," she said.

"Do you like seafood?" he said.

"Well, sure, who doesn't?"

"There's a place...nice seating, not too crowded and the best seafood in town, Interested?" he said.

"Yes, of course. Give me some time to change clothes," she said.

"You look fine to me." Steve surveyed the blue flowered sundress and sandals she wore.

She blushed and brushed the compliment off. "Appreciate your saying that; I'm living out of one suitcase and this is the best it offers. If you think this is okay, that's good enough for me."

She followed him to his pickup, glad to be chauffeured for a change, even if in a work truck.

She was surprised when he pulled the truck into the Gallery parking lot and noticed him watching her.

"Okay, what's going on?" she said.

"You wanted to see the Gallery, right? I decided to combine eating and art tonight - don't argue, just follow me," he said and came around to open her door.

"Yes sir," she said.

He unlocked the glass entry doors and held one open for her. The walls inside the large room were softly lit with recessed lighting that illuminated the paintings and sculptures. Several special sculptural displays of shells and other sea-themed subjects were placed here and there about the floor in mini spots. A large window on the back wall looked out over the Cove and in front of it, was a table-for-two covered in white linen, a bottle of wine and two glasses.

"This is lovely Steve," she said in total surprise. He pulled out a chair and sat opposite her.

A little nervous at being the center of his attention she took in the beautiful paintings in a nearby display. Most were Florida-inspired pieces; native birds, ocean fish and beachscapes, but one caught her eye and she got up to take a closer look.

"Steve, this is yours isn't it?" Then she found his signature in its corner.

"Do you like it?" he said.

"It's the hut on the beach... I think. It's in much better shape than in my dream. When did you paint this?" she said.

"In high school art class when I was about sixteen. Tourists have offered to buy it, but I can't sell; it means too much to me," Steve said.

She turned to meet his eyes for a moment before he led her back to the table and poured the wine.

"To good friends." Steve raised his glass in a toast then asked "Hungry?"

"Yes, I'm starving," Sunnie said. "What's to eat?"

He called out "Enrique" and immediately an older gentleman dressed in a white chef's jacket entered with a tray of appetizers.

"Sunnie, this is Enrique, our chef; Enrique, my guest, Sunnie Reynolds."

"Buenos noches Miss Sunnie," he said. "Welcome to Florida Waters."

"Thank-you, these look very good." There were pink Gulf shrimp lined up like soldiers around a silver bowl with several dipping sauces. Crab puffs with hot sweet and sour sauce shared space with cracked wheat crackers stacked around a pot of smoked mullet spread. She reached for some of everything and deposited them on her plate.

"Since when does a gallery have a chef?" Sunnie said.

"Ah, Mr. Evans hosts many artist receptions during the season and rather than hire caterers, we prepare it right here. Enjoy." Enrique nodded and left the way he came in.

"Ok, this is getting larger than life Steve. You shouldn't have gone to this much expense, I already like you."

"Well in that case, I probably did go a little too far," he said. "Truth be told, it was no expense; Enrique is on the payroll here and at my home."

"You're kidding, right?" she said.

"That large Spanish-style house out on the west edge of the island – it's mine built and paid for."

"Really?" She was amazed and a little flustered. She had him pegged for living the simple life on this tiny island.

"And do you know who's going to buy grandfather's house?" He said.

"I'm going out on a limb here...you?"

"That's affirmative." He smiled and passed her another shrimp basted in orange liquor and coconut milk. "You're the one who started me thinking about keeping the house in the family."

"I know it's none of my business, but how?" Sunnie said.

"It's ok; let's sit down, shall we?" Steve reseated her opposite him.

"Grandfather owned more land than what his house sits on today. His ancestors were among the first on the island and a lot of ocean-front property was passed down to him. He held on to it for years after WWII, but changed as he got older.

"He told my father he realized he was a bitter man; the War clouded his love for his family and he vowed to change. He sold the majority of his land and invested the profits in a trust fund for us. His house and land were given to a relative on a long-term lease with the understanding it would revert to Dad when terminated. Unfortunately, Dad passed away before that happened and it remained in the relative's family.

"Being in real estate, you've probably encountered deals gone wrong at times?" he said.

Sunnie nodded and swallowed her last bite of crab puff. "You would not believe how complicated it can get." She took a sip of her wine.

"I'm sorry," Steve said. "You're hungry and here I am rambling on."

He called again to Enrique who brought lobsters Newberg, a beautiful tossed salad, and crispy hot bread.

They finished their meal as they watched the sun set and leave the night sky to the stars.

"Do you eat like this all the time? I'm absolutely stuffed," she said.

"Enrique keeps me on a strict meat and greens diet through the week," he said.

"Very admirable," she said, thinking of the lunchmeat sandwich she'd devoured the night before.

"Steve, there's something I need to do in order to complete my healing."

"Of course, how can I help?"

"Yesterday, you offered to return to the beach with me. As hard as it is to say, I know I need to go back there and I'd like you by my side, with one caveat;

that you keep me there until I remember everything," Sunnie said. "Are you willing to give this crazy lady another go at it?"

Steve readily agreed to come with her to the old hut. It was a relief to know he'd be there, but Sunnie's fear levels ramped up through the night and falling asleep was hard to do. When she finally did, the nightmare interceded and she awakened with a start as the view of the doorway changed from light to dark.

She sat up and wiped the sweat from her forehead then made her way to the bathroom and took a quick shower. What's the use she thought; I may as well stay awake now.

The sun rose at seven and Sunnie was at the kitchen table with the remains of a Danish pastry. She sighed and poured her second cup of coffee before walking to the library and her computer.

Walter had already emailed his approval for another day on the island, as she knew he would.

Maggie emailed to say hello and wish her good luck with 'the property'. Sunnie hadn't contacted her about developments since she'd discovered the hut. It was too early for doing so in her opinion and too confusing at this point.

Sunnie started the book inventory and spent several hours entering it to computer before she sat down for a nap in the comfy old chair in the library.

She awoke to Steve's voice calling her from the kitchen and walked down the hall.

"Ready to go?" he said from the screen door.

"Let's do this," Sunnie said with false bravado mostly for herself and took his extended hand. They walked together through the sandy yard and started down the path.

"The beach in my dream last night felt familiar for the first time," she said. "I actually knew where I was; it was such a comfort." The tightness in her stomach increased as they approached the shore.

"That's good Sunnie," Steve said. "It sounds like you're making progress."

The sun was dropping toward the western horizon when they stepped onto the sand and walked over to the hut. Steve brought along his machete from the truck and used it to clear the overgrown vines blocking the hut's porch.

Sunnie felt better about the place with Steve there and watched him work with the big knife. She knew it was a day in real time, not the half dream - half reality she'd felt before.

She studied the roof line, high and peaked at its center. There were missing sections to the roof, probably blown off by past hurricanes. She thought it strange that no one had repaired it.

The doorway cleared now, Steve held his hand out to her. "Shall we?"

Sunnie willed her shaky legs to step up to the porch. She looked at the weather-worn boards under her feet; the surreal vision in her dream had provided her no consciousness of the floor's presence.

The sky had turned pink out over the horizon and the sun was still bright enough that they shaded their eyes to look its direction. Sea birds, gulls and pelicans cried their hellos and snatched up their last meals of the day while the tide ebbed. A breeze stirred off the water to cool them and kept mosquitos at bay, at least for the time-being. Sunnie realized that few of these details were in her nightmare.

They walked inside together and found the floor covered with sand from years of storm tides. The fire pit's smoke stains remained on the ceiling above and Steve righted an old bench to sit on.

She looked away to the open door, her eyes pulled there as if by a magnet.

"What is this place Steve and why is it here?" She began to regret her decision to come back.

"When we moved to the island, it was here," he said. "My grandfather used it to be alone; he called it his 'peaceful place'. I wasn't allowed inside, so like any kid told to stay away, I waited until he went out on his fishing boat and came here anyway."

"You lived nearby?" she said and stared as the sun touched the rim of the ocean; its rays still strong enough to pierce the doorway.

"Yes, we lived in the next house down the road." Steve sat beside her. "Grandfather lived alone until his last years."

"What did he look like?" She cast another look at the door where the sun was half gone in the light gray ocean.

"He was tall, very muscular from setting and pulling heavy fishing nets. He had a deep bass voice and wore his hair long." Steve followed Sunnie's line of sight to the door. "What is it?"

"I can't stay here," she said and stood ready to bolt from the room.

"Are you alright?" He touched her shoulder. It was instantly familiar, but she didn't know why.

She stepped away from him, still feeling the warmth where his hand had briefly laid. Then she remembered another time when a young boy had asked the same question... on the very spot where they stood.

Sunnie's knees went weak...*not Steve* she thought; he wouldn't lie...would he?

"I know you," she said. "It was you, wasn't it? You told me never to come here alone because your grandfather would be angry. Did you know me when you came to the house this week? Why did you bring me here and what happened in this place?"

"Sunnie, I know how this looks, but I can explain..."

His eyes were familiar now, their light blue an older version of a young child's face. Then she remembered the painting of the shack at his studio... there was a figure on the steps that didn't click when she looked at it... it was her.

"I can't stay here." She ran through the doorway and heard his footsteps behind as he tried to catch up.

"Sunnie, your name is different and you've changed since we were kids. I didn't recognize you until you told me your dream." He raised his voice to reach her as she ran ahead. "I didn't want to risk telling you before you were ready to handle it."

Something he said hung at the perimeter of her mind, but anger and confusion made it impossible to process. She focused on getting back to the house and climbed the kitchen steps. The door latch was in her hand, but something inside said *no more running* and she turned to confront him.

"I don't know what upsets me more." She yelled into his face and let loose the pent-up anger she'd stockpiled for years.

"You weren't honest enough to level with me or that you're the first to tell me I have a different name. I know nothing about another name and I demand you tell me what it was." She waited with heart beat pounding, unconscious of the tears running down her face.

"It was Sandra; I called you Sandy then," he answered calmly. "Your last name never came up when we were kids. I'm sorry I've made you unhappy, it was never my intent. I wanted to help, that's all."

"I don't believe your lies and you need to go. I'll be leaving in the morning." She pushed through the door and escaped inside, locking it behind her.

Sunnie watched through the curtains in the livingroom as he lingered in the yard looking after her then climbed into his truck and drove away. She didn't remember ever feeling so alone in her life. Apparently there was another time for her on the island.

Chapter Six - Maggie

The next morning, Miami was the same hot and traffic-filled city she'd left three days ago. Sunnie had changed, though it was too early to say just how. She took the interstate straight through to Seashell Realty.

"It's a fantastic piece of property," she said to Walter as they discussed the Decker Island property. She didn't mention Steve or his plan to buy his grandfather's property.

"With a few upgrades like electricity, it'll be a money-maker for certain." She handed him the inventory of the library which she hadn't had a chance to send and he seemed pleased.

"You okay?" Walter said.

"Sure, why do you ask?" she bluffed and turned away to her desk.

"You look different, you feel alright?" He'd never asked her that, so she answered as casually as possible.

"Just a little heat exhaustion I think and the long drive. I'll be fine."

"Well, take the rest of the week off, you've earned it. I'll finish up the paperwork." Walter never volunteered for paperwork and would probably hand it off to Elsy anyway.

"Thanks boss, I appreciate it," she said with more good humor than she felt.

Though Walter had sent her home to rest, she drove in the opposite direction to Maggie's house and parked on the street.

Maggie opened the front door with a smile, but Sunnie's anger had continued to build overnight and now focused on her mother.

"Are you ready to tell me why I've endured this nightmare for years?" she said and Maggie's smile faded.

"You know the story don't you?" Sunnie accused her from the doorway. "Why is my name different?"

"Come in Sunnie," Maggie said calmly, but there were tears in her eyes. Maggie didn't cry about anything, never had. She quickly straightened her shoulders and wiped roughly at her cheek.

She led Sunnie into the livingroom then went to the kitchen for a pitcher of cold lemonade. She soon returned to set the tray upon the coffee table near the sofa, pouring them both a glass full.

"First of all, both your dad and I were instructed by your doctors not to tell you anything you didn't remember," she said. "They told us there could be irreparable damage by doing so. What would you have done in our place?" There was hurt in her eyes.

It made sense to Sunnie; Steve had told her the same thing, but she wasn't ready to be logical yet.

"What's this all about, Mother?" she said.

"I'm going to answer you with a question Sunnie. What brought this up?"

"I've just returned from Decker Island," Sunnie said. "I went on business to size up a new listing. While there, guess who I ran into...Steve Evans."

"Is that Robert Evans' son?" Maggie said. "I wondered if you might figure it out someday, but I didn't see it happening this way." She left the couch to look out the window for a few moments before continuing.

"You went missing on Decker Island for almost ten hours during our vacation. You just disappeared." Maggie was visibly shaken when she turned back to Sunnie.

"Your dad and I were frantic... out of it with worry. As the day passed with no sign of you, the sheriff organized a search party.

"Robert Evans, his wife and father were so kind to us and helped with the search. Darkness fell and there was no moon... a terrible night to search for anyone.

"Around three a.m. there was a knock on our door and Robert's father, a very large and striking elderly man, had you in his arms like a little rag doll. 'It's alright,' he told us. 'She's asleep, I found her in the salt marsh.'

"We were so relieved." Maggie came to sit opposite Sunnie. Her hand shook as she sipped some lemonade.

"Your dad took you and carried you off to your bed while I thanked Mr. Evans over and over again. I offered him a cold drink, food, anything to show how grateful we were, but he said he had to go home.

"When I asked where he found you, he said you were clinging to a log. We never knew why you were there...we were just so glad to find you in one piece.

"By morning, you kept going over and over something about seeing God and he called your name. We thought you were suffering shock from overexposure and dehydration and took you to the mainland hospital. They said there was nothing serious, just mosquito bites and you'd improve soon with food and rest.

"A few weeks after we returned to Miami, you started having nightmares, the same thing over and over. We didn't know what to do and were exhausted from lack of sleep and worry. Your doctor suggested we use your nickname 'Sunnie' instead of Sandra because he thought the sound of your first name could be triggering the dream.

"He's the one who advised against discussing any of it with you. He said you would outgrow whatever shock you'd experienced, so we made the best of it. Your dad and I took turns getting up to comfort you during those first few months," she said.

"I remember that now," Sunnie told her. "You used to say I'd had a nightmare, that it wasn't real and couldn't hurt me. So that's why you changed my name."

"Yes, we even amended your birth records. After a year or so, you started to come back and we thought it was behind us. Then after high school, you started real estate school and you know the rest."

"The dream continued," Sunnie said. "I just didn't tell you and Dad because it upset you both so. With all the arguing between you, I didn't want to add to your problems."

"Ah my dear," Maggie caressed her cheek, "I'm so sorry you've carried the burden by yourself for so long. I wish your father and I could have done better for you, we both felt so helpless. It was our fault for not watching you carefully enough."

Sunnie moved to the couch beside Maggie and put her arm around her shoulders.

"Don't be ridiculous Mom; you both did everything you could, right up to convincing me to start treatment with Dr. Paulding. Last week I finally understood what he was trying to do. I had to stop running away and face whatever happened."

Sunnie released her and thought of Steve. "You remember Steve then? He still lives on the island; he's an artist with his own gallery and works part-time for the island's realty company.

"I didn't recognize him at first until I found the old beach hut. We went back there together yesterday... he tried to help me and I kind of blew up at him..."

"And did you remember what happened?" Maggie said.

"No, I accused him of lying to me and not revealing his identity. He tried to tell me why he did it, to shield me from too much too soon, the same thing the doctors told you.

"Now that you've described our vacation, I do remember snatches of days at the hut. Steve taught me how to catch fish and cook them. He made me laugh after hearing you and dad fighting. He was such a good friend to me."

Sunnie showed Maggie the picture she'd taken of the shack. "It didn't look this bad when we played in it and wasn't scary at all in Steve's painting.

"I still don't know why I have this nightmare, but I'm going to keep after it until I find out the truth."

"I believe you will Sunnie," Maggie said. "And it sounds like you have some bridges to mend, too. We left the island the next day after you were found. We always wondered if Mr. Evans was alright. He was quite old and didn't look well when he left the house."

"I'm going to crash here tonight, okay Mom?" Sunnie felt physically and mentally drained after the long day behind her.

"Of course dear, you know this will always be your home." Maggie's emotions got the best of her again and they hugged before Sunnie walked wearily to her old room.

The next morning, after a shower and change of clothes, Sunnie found Maggie in the kitchen making some breakfast.

"Good morning," Sunnie said and gave Maggie a peck on her cheek. "I'm sorry for barging in here yesterday, you didn't deserve that. I'd had more than I could handle and unfortunately you became a target for all my frustrations."

"I understand dear," Maggie said, "but I should be apologizing to you. You may remember your dad and I had serious problems and most of our vacation was spent arguing. When you disappeared, it made us aware of all our shortfalls as parents; I hope someday you can forgive us."

"Let's put it behind us now, shall we?" Sunnie hugged her again. "I love you, Mom."

"I love you too dear; my heart is full just hearing you say that," Maggie said. "Now, how about some pancakes."

Maggie paused for a second to add, "Call your dad when you get a chance or go see him and tell him what you've found out. I'm sure he'll be relieved. And don't forget to call Dr. Paulding, too."

The next morning Dr. Paulding and Sunnie talked in his office before his first patient.

"So you've explored your mystery? I'm amazed at your courage," he said. "I'm happy for you Sunnie, but do you completely understand what occurred at the hut on the beach?"

"No, and I won't allow myself to stop until I do," she said. "I've met an old friend on the island who helped me walk into the dream so-to-speak and accompanied me. I left before the complete details were clear and I misunderstood his motive in not revealing himself as a childhood friend; he was worried he might upset me.

"My mother said my first pediatric counselor told her and dad not to discuss the dream with me and to change my name as a possible trigger," Sunnie said.

"I'm not surprised at the method," Dr. Paulding said. "It was a popular way of dealing with childhood trauma at the time; things have improved in the profession since those days. Individual differences are now considered, such as coping mechanisms, family stressors and age-related vulnerabilities; they all determine how a child reacts to fear."

"It's due to your influence and confidence in my 'competent brain' that I remain inspired to take action, so please, no regrets for either of us," Sunnie said. "My mother supplied a lot of the backstory last night. We've reconciled... her and me."

"I'm happy to hear that, Sunnie. Then don't wait too long," he advised. "Use your momentum to finish this up and clear the way for life. You've lived too long in the past's shadows."

Sunnie checked in at Seashell Realty later in the morning; obviously Walter had been worried over her haggard look upon return from Decker Island. His face lit up at seeing her walk in.

"You're back, but I gave you the week off!"

"I know and I feel much better after a good night's sleep," she said.

"I read over the notes you sent and already received a call from a potential buyer who intends to file for a historical grant on the property," Walter said.

"That's great, but what's historical about it?" She put down her purse, waved at Elsy and walked over to sit at his desk.

"It was built by the first inhabitant of the island and his grandson, a WWII hero, lived there, too. It looks pretty good for approval by the National Historical Society," Walter said.

There's more to this story Sunnie thought; Steve's grandfather must be the hero Walter's talking about.

"Boss, can I take you up on that offer for a week off? There's something I have to take care of," she said.

"But you just got here," Walter said. He tried his usual solemn approach, but noticed her large-eyed look. "Oh heck – you're due some vacation time anyway – get outta here." He waved a hand her direction so she grabbed her bag and headed for the door.

"Sunnie, you're rushing off already?" Elsy said. "Sorry I couldn't find that info you requested."

"That's okay Elsy, thanks for looking for the needle in a haystack anyway," Sunnie said. Elsy's face grew a little uncertain at the old adage's meaning.

"See you next week and I'll tell you what that means," Sunnie said.

Sunnie turned to Walter before dodging out the door and gave him a salute. "Thanks Boss!" she called from outside before the door slammed.

Elsy looked to Walter for an explanation, but he just shrugged his shoulders and returned to his computer.

Chapter Seven – The Last Fear

The drive to Decker Island felt longer, perhaps because Sunnie now had two missions she was anxious to complete; one was to face the mystery of the hut and the second was to see Steve again and apologize.

Thankfully, alligators and locusts were again missing from her itinerary; she was two for two, how lucky could she get?

She arrived at Island Realty by 3 pm and pulled in just as Millie was leaving the office.

"Hi, how are you?" Sunnie said, a little over the top on cheerfulness.

"Sunnie? I'm fine - what are you doing here," Millie said, a little surprised to see her.

"I have some unfinished business, glad to hear we may have a deal on the house, by the way," Sunnie said.

"Oh yes, me too," Millie's eyebrows rose as if she were puzzled.

"Do you know where Steve is?" Sunnie forged ahead.

"Why, he's at the house doing some repair and painting," Millie said with a tilt of her head.

"Thank-you, have a great day," Sunnie said.

"Yes, you too dear..." Sunnie had jumped back into her car before Millie could finish her sentence; she'd wanted to ask if Sunnie knew Steve was the buyer for the house.

Steve was at the top of the ladder painting the siding when Sunnie drove slowly up the two-rut driveway. She was happy the new color matched the original traces of blue left on the building.

He turned around with brush suspended mid-air to stare until her car closed the distance. Sunnie could tell the moment he recognized her and turned back to his painting.

So that's how it is she thought; looks like I have a big bridge to mend. At that moment, a gaggle of ibis chose to dart from the weeds and sped on their way in front of the car. She braked for them then parked.

At the bottom of the ladder, she called out "Hey there. How are you?"

"I'm fine, thank-you." Steve said and continued his painting.

She realized this was not going to be easy.

"Can you forgive a crazy lady?" she said. He certainly had a lot to forgive and now she wondered if he would.

He hesitated a moment with the brush, but then continued. "I don't know. You registered some pretty serious accusations last time we talked."

Time for confession she thought.

"Yes, I did and you deserved none of them," Sunnie said.

"I'm glad you realize that," he said and dipped his brush again into the paint can.

"What can I do to make it up to you Steve?" she said.

At last he put the brush down and began his descent. At ground level again, he pulled out a rag from his back pocket and wiped his hands. Only then did he look directly at her and her heart felt heavy. This is not going well is it she acknowledged to herself.

"Let's sit on the porch Sunnie," he said and walked ahead.

She sat on the swing and he dragged up a chair.

"Here's the thing Sunnie. I probably had a child's eye view of the way it was when we were younger. But we're adults now and time has taught us each its lessons and made us what we are today. Do you agree?"

"Yes, I do, but..." Sunnie stopped when he held up his hand.

"Please, let me get through this," he said. "I'll always remember our time at the beach as one of the happiest in my life. But, because we're different now, I have no patience for misunderstandings and distrust in a relationship. I'm at the age where I feel the years moving by, my dues are paid and I'll wait for the person who feels the same."

"I understand Steve and I respect you for telling me," Sunnie said. "I hope someday we can at least be friends again." He began to turn away and she continued.

"I have more than a few loose ends to tie up here before I leave, but I don't expect any more of your time and I mean that. I do want to thank-you for everything you've done and for helping me to push through some hard times. It was invaluable and I will never be able to repay you." She walked around him to the steps and down to the car.

Steve watched as she drove away and thought about it. He still came to the same truth and couldn't take back a word of what he'd said.

Sunnie drove to the mainland and a motel. The loss of Steve as a friend was hard, but she would not give up on herself, she'd come too far to do so.

It was three-thirty in the afternoon and she watched television for a while then took a nap. Her phone alarm went off at six p.m.

She remained stronger than ever after the past few days' revelations and would face the last deficit in her memory...alone.

Her timing was good; Steve had left the house so she pulled up the driveway and parked the car out of sight from the street. She walked to the backyard and the beach path.

The sun was on its way to the horizon when she reached the sand; familiar with her surroundings now, she knew what to expect at this point and for the time-being, her fear was minimal.

She walked to the hut and straight inside the sandy-floored room. She sat on the bench and purposely faced the door.

As the sun completed its descent and touched the horizon in the Gulf, its bright rays beamed through the doorway and she waited. The sound of the high tide resonated in the room, waves crashed and gulls cried out as they fed on small fish and mollusks.

The stage was set for the shadow fear, a left over from all the other fears she'd resolved. A familiar tightness in her stomach heralded her fight or flight response Dr. Paulding had described to her, but she chose to stay and fight.

Sunnie purposely recalled the details she already knew; the fire pit with its glowing coals and the fish cooking just there. The sun's brightness... the wind blowing strongly and the shadow that waited just outside... always threatening but never materializing.

The setting sun moved to its last few inches above the edge of the earth and the ocean breeze picked up; still she watched the door, ready to see.

Footsteps came across the porch and she entered a portion of memory that had been blocked away since childhood.

She was now caught in the dream. Like a sandpiper under an oncoming wave she felt its presence above her and a thousand warnings went off in her brain. Still, her eyes were held to the doorway.

A moving form had suddenly blocked the sun. He was tall; his long white hair flew wildly in the wind, backlit and illuminated by the light out on the horizon.

She heard the deep baritone voice.

SANDRA! YOU DON'T BELONG HERE!

The ten year old child had panicked and unreasoned terror came upon her, for she believed it was God and he was displeased with her. Mommy and daddy were getting a divorce… it was all her fault.

Sunnie wrapped her arms around her shoulders and kept watching the shadow… she remembered now.

The child had run like a frightened rabbit through an opening in the back wall, straight into the tide-water marsh where she'd climbed behind a fallen tree to hide. She'd watched for hours to see if God would find her and cried for her mommy and daddy, but they never came.

Tears streamed down Sunnie's face over this last revelation. She cried for that little girl; too young to hear her parents' talk of leaving each other, she'd accepted the blame as her own.

She cried for the years of nightmares and a child's secret perception of an angry God buried deep within her all this time.

Everything remembered washed over her in one massive, incoming wave and she drowned in the needless waste of it all until its weight finally ebbed and her tears, guilt, grief and fear were swept away.

The sun had left the sky and Sunnie was alone in the hut's dusky light.

Steve entered the doorway and saw her on the bench.

"Sunnie?" he called softly.

She recognized his voice. "Steve? I thought you were your grandfather."

He couldn't help himself and walked closer. "Was he here?"

"Yes, but only in my mind," she said and smiled at him.

Chapter Eight - Restart

Last night as they walked on the beach Steve stopped to point out a bright shooting star, its wide trail extended and followed it for several seconds. He said it was probably space trash hitting the atmosphere, but Sunnie preferred to think it was a real star and made a wish upon it.

This morning she lay in bed half-awake at the old island house and had decided to take a day for relaxation and drive back to Miami tomorrow.

She turned over to watch the sun slowly light the yard outside. Birds were already busy in the palms beside her bedroom window and searched for small lizards and their eggs hidden in the recesses of the palm's fronds.

Seagulls cried as they passed over the house on their way to the shore. It was a welcome sound to wake to and Sunnie did so without her usual fear.

She sat up - "Without fear!" she exclaimed.

Sunnie was suddenly, wonderfully awake. The beach didn't frighten her anymore; she could go there whenever she wanted.

It was surreal to feel as she did. Revelations of the past few days came one by one and clicked through her mind in orderly fashion. She was now in control and no longer needed them, but would repeat them for Dr. Paulding at a later date.

She felt rested and without her usual headache, a different person from the woman who had returned to the Island yesterday.

As she swung her legs over the side of the bed, it hit her... there was no nightmare last night.

So this is what it was to be 'normal' she thought and hugged her pillow before throwing it into the air.

She took a few moments to thank God for guiding her safely to this time in her life then jumped out of bed to get dressed.

After breakfast, Sunnie dropped into the big comfortable chair in the library to finish Alice's Adventures.

It was still early when she closed the book and her eyes drifted to the new cache of books she'd found during her inventory, pirates in the Gulf of Mexico.

Being on the island had fueled her interest in pirates. The morning passed her unawares as she sailed the Caribbean into the Gulf with the likes of Jean Lafitte and Calico Jack Rackum.

Waves on the shore earlier had announced a high tide and she knew when it ebbed, the shelling would be the best. She slipped into sandals and grabbed a plastic bag in the kitchen before pushing through the screen door

The sandy, now-familiar path to the beach felt like her magic carpet to ride. Her feet were light, her heart open to anything the day might present. The prickly little seed pods scattered across her path from the gum trees overhead even brought back a childhood memory. She and Maggie had gathered the pods until their pockets were full and made little owls out of them, using beads for eyes and gluing them to a shell base.

Within an hour of her beach stroll, Sunnie had filled the bag with white scallop shells, veiled eyes, rooster conchs, small trumpet shells and pieces of coral.

Her favorites were the transparent shells in white, yellow, pale orange and silver. Maggie had named them 'jingle shells' because when you shook them in your hand, they gave off a faint jingle, like fairy coins. They never knew what the shells were really called. She decided to take the bag to Maggie as a surprise when she returned to Miami.

The old, broken-down hut at the edge of the jungle held no threat for her now. She paused in front of it to reflect on its meaning in her life, the happier times with Steve and a child's fear that culminated there. The wind-worn structure had held on until she could return to discover its secrets and she was grateful.

Steve came onto the beach and Sunnie waved.

"Aren't you the beachcomber," he said and examined the bag of shells hanging at her side.

"Yes, freedom is a wonderful thing," she said. "I was just heading back, shall we walk?"

"Good idea since some guy delivered a mess of shrimp and salad to the kitchen table," he said.

"Some guy, eh?" Sunnie said. "Might it have been that plumber/artist who lives at the end of the Island?"

"Might be," he said. "I thought you'd be here now that the old hut's secrets are out."

He stopped walking and turned to her. "Sunnie, I want to tell you how sorry I am about the way I reacted when you returned yesterday, and that you had to come alone to the hut. I'm not proud of it... can you forgive me?"

"There's nothing to forgive, Steve. You did what you felt was right. In fact, you enabled me to forge ahead on my own. Do you know how good that feels?" She spread her arms and almost dropped the shells.

"So, letting it out is good; holding it in is bad?" He took the bag to carry.

"Now you have it my friend," Sunnie said. "I'd lived life defined by a nameless fear, it was time for me to stand and face it, so thank-you for speeding up the process."

They hugged until Sunnie laughed.

"I suddenly have a hunger for shrimp. Race you back!" She started running with Steve close behind.

"I'll put the plates out and you get the tea," Sunnie said after they reached the kitchen. "There's something I still don't understand. Last night you talked about your grandfather's bitterness after the war; what did you mean?"

"Have you heard of the Bataan death march?" Steve said. "Grandfather served in the Pacific theatre during 1942 and was taken prisoner when the island of Luzon fell. They marched the prisoners 65 miles to a train for Camp O'Donnell; eleven days and nights without food and drinking from puddles. Less than half of the men made it alive. Those who didn't had their dog tags removed and were left for those behind to walk around."

"Dear God." Sunnie stopped setting the table for a moment to look at him.

"Only 250 Americans survived," Steve said. "Grandfather received honors for saving many men by stealing garbage and smuggling it to them. I didn't know anything about it until dad sat me down one day."

He put two glasses out and went to the fridge for the jug of tea.

"I'd been avoiding grandfather and thought he didn't love me, he was grouchy so much of the time. I never imagined what war was like until that day. That's why he came here to the hut to meditate."

"He must have relived it over and over," Sunnie said. "I can relate to that; he had post-traumatic stress syndrome."

They sat down to dinner and began pulling the sweet gulf shrimp from their shells.

"What did happen to you Sunnie?" Steve said. "I've never known exactly what transpired."

"I can tell you more about it than I've ever known," she said.

"It was your grandfather in the doorway; I know that from your description of him. His deep voice called me 'Sandra' and I believed he was God. He told me I didn't belong there," Sunnie said. "That's why my first name always triggered the nightmare."

They ate the shrimp dipped in a red sauce laced with horseradish, lime juice, and a few drops of Louisiana-style hot sauce. She passed some garlic bread to Steve before she continued.

"I was a timid, overly sheltered child and the "special effects" of wind, light and his deep voice had me convinced he was a divine being. The terror I felt at seeing him, stayed all these years."

"And do you know the reason now?" Steve said.

"It was something I was unaware of before. I'd heard my parents' frequent arguments for years; it stressed me more than they ever knew. When I heard them talk of divorce, I took all the blame on myself and truly thought God blamed me, too."

"How do you feel now?" Steve said.

"I know neither of my parents ever blamed me. It was a conclusion drawn by a child who saw her world falling apart," Sunnie said.

After dinner and dishes, they sat together on the front porch and sipped brandy brought from the library.

"I remember something, too and didn't connect it until now," Steve said. "I overheard Grandfather telling dad he'd frightened someone and the person ran away. He'd helped search thru the night and shined his truck lights across a marsh as a last effort. It had to be you he found draped over a log asleep and carried out, straight to your parents."

"I don't remember much about the next morning except being covered with mosquito bites," she said.

"Sunnie, I think you were the influence for my grandfather's epiphany," Steve said thoughtfully. "The way you perceived him that day shook him and he knew he'd turned into someone he didn't like. It was enough to bring him out of his nightmare and back to us. Strange as it sounds, he became the gentle and kind grandfather I'd always wanted."

"I'm sure you're right, Steve," Sunnie said. "It was an unfortunate perception of him by a very scared little girl and I harbor no animosity for him or his memory."

An owl disturbed the silence with his 'whoo-whoo' then flew out to find his mate who answered. Tree frogs sang in various voices as they waited for flying insects to enter their perch on the wall under the porch light.

"It's the end of the story, isn't it?" Sunnie said quietly. "All mysteries solved, questions answered and lessons learned."

"And what lessons have you learned?" Steve said as he put an arm around her shoulders.

"Well, that some things in life are not always as we remember and terrors left alone can grow out of proportion rather than fade as the years go by. Better to face them." She leaned against him for a while and listened to the breeze in the night's songs.

"Let's talk about this old house," Steve said and roused from her side to lean against the porch railing. "I'm planning to dedicate this place to my grandfather along with the island's men and women who served in the military. I'll preserve what's here now so that future generations can see how the island's culture began."

"It's a wonderful idea," Sunnie said.

"I also plan to build a small museum," he said then his eyes widened. "Do you know there's a rumor that pirates frequently visited here?"

"You have no idea how much I know." She laughed at the look on his face. "I'm totally into the pirate section of your library and I think it'll be a fantastic addition."

"I'm offering you the Curator position Sunnie, please stay," he said.

"Steve, I'm flattered, but I'm no historian."

"You're smart, organized and I sense, too that you love the island," he said. "Besides, you come highly recommended."

"What do you mean?" She said.

"I happened to talk to your boss, Walter, yesterday. He's quite the character witness on your behalf and loves the job you've done for him."

"You're very thorough, aren't you?" She said.

"Yes, I guess I am, but I'd do the same for anyone I intended to bring here. You're special Sunnie and the museum needs you. I have enough on my plate with my art, the Gallery and the real estate company, yes, it's mine too." He answered the look of surprise on her face.

"I want to stay involved, but I promise you'll have free rein; what do you say?" He said.

Steve was so hopeful that Sunnie had to ask; "What's the other reason you want me here?"

He tried to keep a straight face, but she continued to wait for an answer. He took her hands and pulled her from the swing.

"Sunnie, I've loved you since we were kids. I want you close enough to get to know you again."

With his confession Sunnie also recognized something about herself.

"I think…I'm not ready." She stepped back. "For the first time in life I'm free of the thing that's always held me back. I don't want to become a permanent part of anything at this point. Can you understand that?" She said softly.

He touched her cheek for a moment then dropped his hand. "It's not what I hoped for, but yes, I do understand. When will you leave?"

"I'll drive back in the morning." The smile left his face and he was so forlorn that she gave him one last hug.

"You'll always be in my heart," she said.

The next morning Sunnie turned her car towards Miami then glanced down at the eleven yellow roses on the seat beside her. Steve brought them just as she'd prepared to leave the house.

He said what she already knew. "My life is on this island, Sunnie. Go do and be happy. If you ever tire of wandering, I hope you'll come back here."

Epilogue - Bronx, New York 2018

Three years ago, Sunnie wasn't sure if she would make it in the City, it was so totally different from Miami. Traffic bustled, horns sounded, the 'el' ran overhead; the sounds of the city were a combination of its people and the machines they moved; bicycles, scooters, cars, buses, cabs, trucks, and trains.

The hardest adjustment for her was the way people walked by, each on their own mission; they greeted no one unless they knew each other.

In the beginning she spent weeks getting oriented to trains and buses. But gradually she learned what to expect and found the places she loved; among them, the Bronx Zoo and the amazing architecture of Washington Park.

Life was good in New York now. Sunnie traveled abroad whenever work allowed and during the first year she joined two other realtors to manage an apartment rental service. Maggie still had a sister living in New York City who helped by listing her apartment with Sunnie's company.

Owning her own business had been one of Sunnie's primary goals and the company grew steadily. By her second year of city living she let her own small apartment without benefit of a roommate's income.

One day, while walking home from the bus stop after a shopping expedition, she noticed a poster in a florist's window and stopped to read it.

The words took her by surprise and seemed to be a profound reference to Steve's when he gave her flowers and wished her well. She suddenly felt weak in the knees and walked into a deli next door to grab a coffee.

She sat on a stool at the window and watched people go by. It was September and leaves had begun to turn color, some already collected into piles on the sidewalk and across the street on the park lawns. She missed the South since winter would soon follow and she was not a snow person.

The rewards of the move had come at a price. No matter how many interesting people she'd met, she was alone. The life she dreamed of during her fear-ridden years had not yielded one person with the wit, positivity and creativeness of Steve. And no one had made her feel the same as when they were together.

She finished her coffee and continued home to her apartment.

During her first year in New York, she and Steve called each other regularly, but the longer apart, the longer the time between calls. She was distracted with being her own person and gradually drifted toward life between her three story walkup and the office downtown.

At the apartment building, she dug into her ginormous bag for keys to the lobby then ascended the stairs. As she cleared the last step on the third floor she turned the corner into the hallway.

Someone was leaning against the wall in front of her door. She unconsciously gripped the pepper spray canister attached to her key chain and slowed her steps. Then she laughed as she recognized him and walked full speed into Steve's arms.

He twirled her around until she was dizzy. "Put me down, puleez," she begged. He laughed and stopped the spinning. They looked at each other for a long time, each waiting to see what the other would say. He finally went first.

"How are you?"

"Fine; what are you doing here?" she said.

"I had some business in the City and decided to look for you; Walter spilled your new address."

She was speechless and they continued to stare at each other.

"Are you going to invite me in or shall I leave?" he said.

"Yes...no, I mean, don't leave – please, come in." She made a few awkward stabs at the lock with the key until he finally relieved her of it and opened the door. She put her purse on the hall table and picked up the mail from the floor as he walked past into the livingroom.

"This looks familiar." He faced the painting over the breakfast table; an island seascape he'd tucked into the backseat of her car before seeing her off with flowers that last morning.

"Yes," Sunnie told him, "it reminds me where my life restarted. Would you like something, a soda or water?"

"No thank-you," he turned toward her, "I can't stay; my plane..."

"Oh," she said, diminished by his words. "Of course, I understand."

"Do you?" he said. "I've been thinking about you and hoped you were happy and making it in the big city."

They sat and she briefly shared her life since leaving the island; he smiled when she finished.

"Good, I'm glad Sunnie. You were so eager to fly free and it looks like you're doing what you set out to do." He stood and prepared to leave.

"You're really leaving already?" she said.

"Yes, my plane leaves in an hour and a half. You never know what traffic can dish up here, so I'd better go." He took her in his arms and held her; she remembered being there before and it was like being home again.

"Take care of yourself," he said and stooped to pick up his brief case.

"I will and you do the same. Wonderful to see you Steve, thanks so much for stopping by."

Could we get any more formal she thought as she closed the door behind him and leaned against it.

What just happened here? Didn't I spend an hour in a deli today deciding I missed him enough to call him? The thought jumped on her and she realized... *I feel like going after him.* Should I? Is this really what I want?

In a split second she was out of her apartment and headed down the stairwell. At the first landing she turned the corner and fairly ran right into him.

"What are you doing?" they said at the same time and laughed.

"I don't want you to go," she said, short of breath from the stairs.

"I don't want to leave," he said, closing the distance between them to kiss her.

The only thing left to do at this point was to find level ground... and avoid falling down the stairwell. Sunnie definitely and positively kissed him right back.

Yellow Flowers mean:

Joy, Gladness,
Friendship, Delight,
A Promise of a new
beginning.
Remember me,
Welcome back,
I Care.

Author Bio – Reboot 2019

The author has filled many roles in life: as a nurse tech for senior care, a yeoman in the U.S. Navy during the Vietnam War, a needle-arts manager and instructor, a sewing machine repair tech, an artist in acrylics and pastels, and as a healthcare risk manager. She never predicted that her writing hobby would be recognized someday; it was merely a way to escape stress in the work-world.

Her first nationally published story for Country magazine changed that and put her on a road to create her biography/ family history, Ohio Girl. Five fiction novels soon followed.

"People we meet teach us the value of the human spirit – and with each there is something learned as we cross paths. That's why I write stories about the power to push through negatives in life. Perhaps someday people will say that my beliefs are contained in the stories, and that will be enough for this writer." *Linda J Pifer*